CLASSROOM CRITTERS

A NEW YEAR

by Molly Beth Griffin
illustrated by Colin Jack

KT-872-352

C334402132

CONTENTS

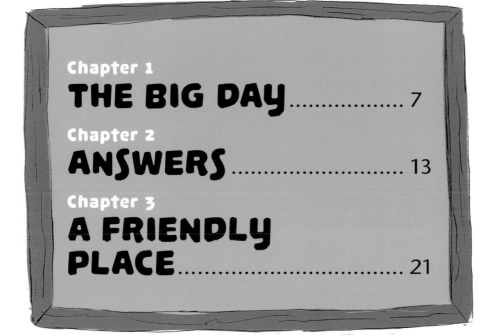

CLASSROOM CRITTERS

These five friends live within the walls, nooks and crannies of a primary school. They learn alongside the children every day, even though the children don't see them!

STELLA

Stella is a mouse. She loves her friends. She also loves children and school! She came into the school on a cold winter's day. She knew it would be her home forever. Her favourite subjects are history and music. She is always eager for a new day to start.

BO

Bo is a parakeet. He is a classroom pet. The friends let him out of his cage so they can play together. Bo loves to read. He goes home with his teacher at the weekend, but he always comes back to school to see his friends.

DELILAH

Delilah is a spider. She has always lived in the corners of the school. She is so small the children never notice her, but she is very clever. Delilah loves maths and computers and hates the broom!

NICO

Nico is a toad. He used to be a classroom pet. A child forgot to put him back into his tank one day. Now he lives with his friends. The whole school is his home! He can be grumpy, but he loves science and art. As Nico doesn't have fingers, he paints with his toes!

GOLDIE

Goldie is a goldfish. She is very wise. The friends ask her questions when they have a big decision to make. She gives good advice and lives in the library.

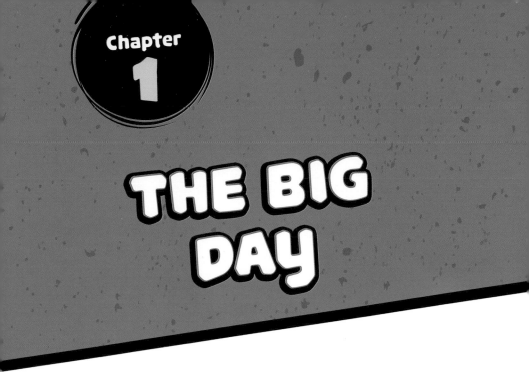

THE BIG DAY

At last! The sun rose on the first day of school after the summer holidays. Stella the Mouse was so excited!

"Wake up! Wake up! Wake up!" she called to her friends.

Nico the Toad grumbled. Delilah the Spider yawned. Bo the Parakeet ruffled his feathers.

"The children come back today," said Stella. "Get up! Get up! Get up!"

Nico, Delilah and Bo stretched. Then they got up and joined Stella. Now that they were awake, they were excited too.

"Let's go! Let's go! Let's go!" squeaked Stella.

The friends rushed to the doors. Children poured off the school buses. They wore new autumn clothes. They carried bright backpacks and lunchboxes.

Their shoes clomped down the corridor. Loud chatter filled the air.

The kids were just as excited as
Stella about starting a new year!

Well, most of the kids were
excited. One girl scuffed her shoes
along the corridor. Another boy
dragged his new backpack.

"That girl looks sad," said Nico.

"That boy does too," said
Delilah.

"I think some of the children are worried," said Bo.

"But why? School is WONDERFUL!" Stella said.

"Maybe they don't know that yet," said Bo.

"Do you think maybe they are new?" Stella asked.

Her friends shrugged. They didn't know.

But they did know where to go if they had questions. They rushed to the library to ask Goldie.

Chapter 2

ANSWERS

"Are there new kids at school today?" Stella asked.

Goldie looked at Stella and swam in a circle.

"Blub," she said.

One blub meant yes and two blubs meant no. At least that's what the friends thought she was saying.

"But Goldie, new things are exciting! Shouldn't those new kids be happy to be at school?" Stella asked.

"Blub, blub."

"No?" Stella was confused. She sat down to think.

"I remember the first day I got out of my tank," said Nico. "I had been wanting to escape for so long. But then once I was out, it was scary. I couldn't find my way around."

"Yes," said Delilah. "The school seemed very big and loud when I first hatched from my egg. I was nervous and worried."

"When my teacher first brought me to school, I hid in the corner of my cage all day. All the kids were looking at me. I felt so shy," Bo said.

"Do you remember your first day at school, Stella?" asked Delilah. "Weren't you scared?"

Stella thought about it. She remembered being hungry outside. She remembered being cold. Stella also remembered how dark it was out there.

But when Stella crawled through the small crack in the bricks, she was no longer scared.

"The school was warm and bright and full of food," Stella said.

"You weren't scared? Ever?" asked Nico.

"Or nervous? Or worried?" asked Delilah.

"Or shy?" asked Bo.

"Well, I do remember being scared I was going to get stepped on. I remember worrying about the broom. I remember wishing for a friend," Stella said.

She looked around at Nico, Delilah and Bo.

"Having friends made me brave," Stella said.

Stella knew what she had to do.

Chapter 3

A FRIENDLY PLACE

Stella told her friends the plan. They were just as excited as Stella and got to work straight away!

They scurried, hopped, crept and fluttered round the school. They carried paper, paint, glue, pens and glitter.

It took some time, but Stella found all the children who looked sad, scared or worried.

She listened in on their lessons and learnt their names.

Nico loved to paint. He painted hearts and flowers.

Bo loved to write. He wrote kind words and poems.

Delilah folded the notes into beautiful shapes.

Together, they dropped the surprises into the backpacks of the new kids. Then they waited and watched.

It was hard for the animals to stay hidden. They were excited about making the children happy.

They waited. And waited. And waited. It felt like forever, but the last bell finally rang.

The children rushed out of the classrooms. Their shoes clomped down the corridor. Loud chatter filled the air again.

The first day of school had finished. The teachers and children looked relieved.

When the children packed up to go home, they found the notes. They smiled.

They looked around, wondering who was being so nice to them. They couldn't see anyone, but they kept smiling.

Then they walked to the front doors and out into the sunny autumn day.

They did not scuff their feet or drag their backpacks.

"The new kids look so much happier!" said Nico.

"They might still be a bit sad or scared or worried," said Bo.

"But now they know school can be a warm, bright place," said Stella. "A friendly place."

Stella, Nico, Delilah and Bo waved goodbye.

"Now all the children can be excited about the new year," Stella said to her friends. "Just like me!"

TALK ABOUT IT

1. The five animals in this story are best friends. They call themselves the Classroom Critters. What would you call your group of friends?

2. What is your favourite part of a new school year?

3. Do you think teachers get nervous about a new school year? Why or why not?

WRITE ABOUT IT

1. The first day of school can make you feel lots of different emotions. Write a paragraph about how you felt on your first day of school.

2. Make a list of things you could do to help a friend who is feeling sad.

3. There are many adjectives used to describe how the animals move throughout the story. Find at least three movement words and use them in a short story.

MOLLY BETH GRIFFIN

Molly Beth Griffin is a writing teacher at the Loft Literary Center in Minneapolis, Minnesota, USA. She has written numerous picture books (including *Loon Baby* and *Rhoda's Rock Hunt*) and a YA novel (*Silhouette of a Sparrow*). Molly loves reading and hiking in all kinds of weather. She lives in South Minneapolis with her partner and two children.

COLIN JACK

Colin Jack has illustrated several books for children, including *Little Miss Muffet* (Flip-Side Rhymes), *Jack and Jill* (Flip-Side Rhymes), *Dragons from Mars*, *7 Days of Awesome* and *If You Happen to Have a Dinosaur*. He also works as a story artist and character designer at DreamWorks Studios. Colin splits his time living in California, USA, and Canada with his wife and two children.

Raintree is an imprint of Capstone Global Library Limited, a company
incorporated in England and Wales having its registered office at 264
Banbury Road, Oxford, OX2 7DY – Registered company number: 6695582

www.raintree.co.uk
myorders@raintree.co.uk

Text © Capstone Global Library Limited 2020
The moral rights of the proprietor have been asserted.

All rights reserved. No part of this publication may be reproduced in any
form or by any means (including photocopying or storing it in any medium
by electronic means and whether or not transiently or incidentally to some
other use of this publication) without the written permission of the copyright
owner, except in accordance with the provisions of the Copyright, Designs
and Patents Act 1988 or under the terms of a licence issued by the Copyright
Licensing Agency, Barnard's Inn, 86 Fetter Lane, London, EC4A 1EN (www.
cla.co.uk). Applications for the copyright owner's written permission should
be addressed to the publisher.

Illustrated by Colin Jack
Designed by Ted Williams

Shutterstock: AVA Bitter, design element throughout,
Oleksandr Rybitskiy, design element throughout

Original illustrations © Capstone Global Library Limited 2020
Originated by Capstone Global Library Ltd
Printed and bound in India

ISBN 978 1 4747 7180 1

British Library Cataloguing in Publication Data:
A full catalogue record for this book is available from the British Library.